AMAZON BEST-SELLING AUTHOR
WRITTEN BY SHAI
a familiar
AURA
THE HEART NEVER FORGETS

a familiar AURA

THE HEART NEVER FORGETS

Published by Stepping Stones Publishing
Copyright © Shai

PAPERBACK *ISBN: 978-1-915862-13-6*
*HARDBACK **ISBN: 978-1-915862-14-3***

SCAN THIS QR
CODE TO UNLOCK
THE AURA PLAYLIST

AALiYAH (24)

a familiar AURA

CHAPTER 1

AS I LEFT MY LIFE AND FRIENDS BEHIND IN LONDON, I COULDN'T HELP BUT FEEL A TWINGE OF SADNESS. BUT THE OPPORTUNITY TO PURSUE MY DREAMS IN SEOUL WAS TOO GOOD TO PASS UP. AS I ARRIVED IN SEOUL, I IMMEDIATELY FELT A SENSE OF EXCITEMENT AND FAMILIARITY. AS A HALF-KOREAN, I HAD ALWAYS FELT A STRONG CONNECTION TO MY HERITAGE, AND BEING IN KOREA BROUGHT BACK MEMORIES OF MY CHILDHOOD VISITS TO MY GRANDMA'S HOUSE.

BUT AS I STARTED TO NAVIGATE MY NEW LIFE IN SEOUL, I QUICKLY REALISED THAT THERE WERE TO BE MANY CHALLENGES FOR ME TO OVERCOME. ONE OF THE BIGGEST CHALLENGES FOR ME, WAS THE FACT THAT I HAD ALWAYS GROWN UP FEELING KOREAN AND BEING TREATED AS A KOREAN BACK IN LONDON BUT HERE I'M TREATED LIKE A FOREIGNER... IT'S COMPLICATED, NEVER TRULY FEELING LIKE YOU BELONG IN PLACES THAT SHOULD BE YOUR HOME...

NOT TO MENTION THAT LIVING ALONE FOR THE FIRST TIME WAS BOTH EXCITING AND DAUNTING, AND I HAD TO GET USED TO THE NEW ROUTINE OF TAKING CARE OF MYSELF.

NOT TO MENTION THAT
THIS WOULD BE MY FIRST TIME
BACK SINCE THE ACCIDENT…

DESPITE THESE CHALLENGES, I WAS DETERMINED TO MAKE THE MOST OF MY TIME IN SEOUL. I WAS SET TO MOVE INTO MY NEW APARTMENT NOT FAR FROM GANGNAM TRAIN STATION, AND I COULDN'T WAIT TO MAKE IT MY OWN.

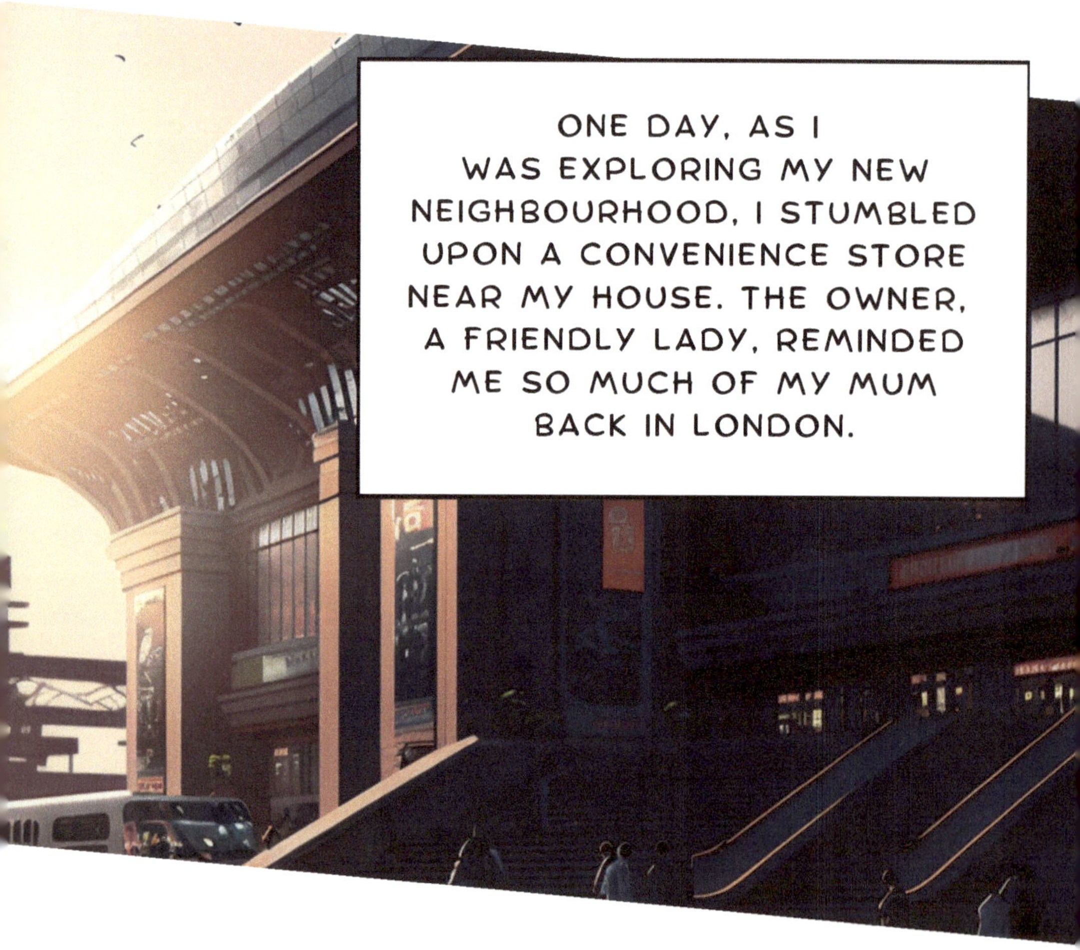

ONE DAY, AS I WAS EXPLORING MY NEW NEIGHBOURHOOD, I STUMBLED UPON A CONVENIENCE STORE NEAR MY HOUSE. THE OWNER, A FRIENDLY LADY, REMINDED ME SO MUCH OF MY MUM BACK IN LONDON.

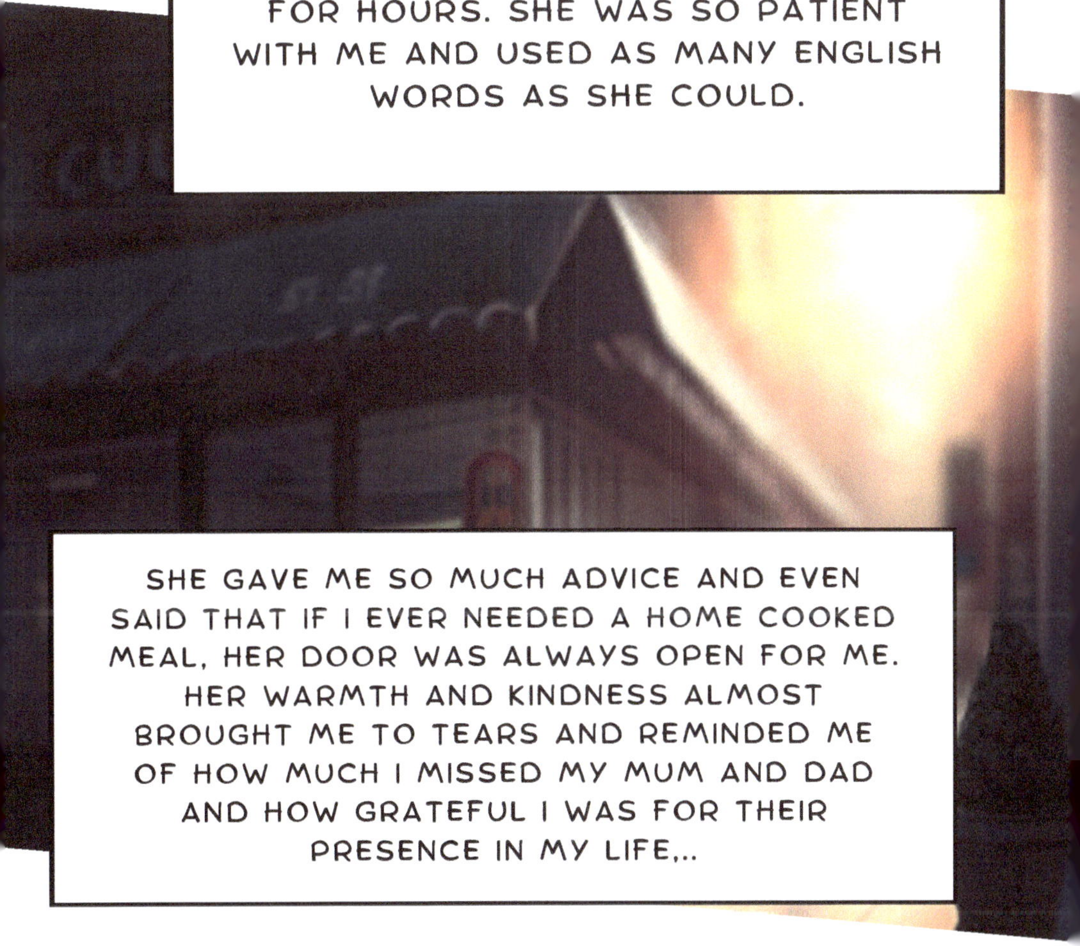

WE STRUCK UP A CONVERSATION AND I FOUND MYSELF CHATTING WITH HER FOR HOURS. SHE WAS SO PATIENT WITH ME AND USED AS MANY ENGLISH WORDS AS SHE COULD.

SHE GAVE ME SO MUCH ADVICE AND EVEN SAID THAT IF I EVER NEEDED A HOME COOKED MEAL, HER DOOR WAS ALWAYS OPEN FOR ME. HER WARMTH AND KINDNESS ALMOST BROUGHT ME TO TEARS AND REMINDED ME OF HOW MUCH I MISSED MY MUM AND DAD AND HOW GRATEFUL I WAS FOR THEIR PRESENCE IN MY LIFE,..

*HOME: AALIYAH IS REFERRING TO LONDON

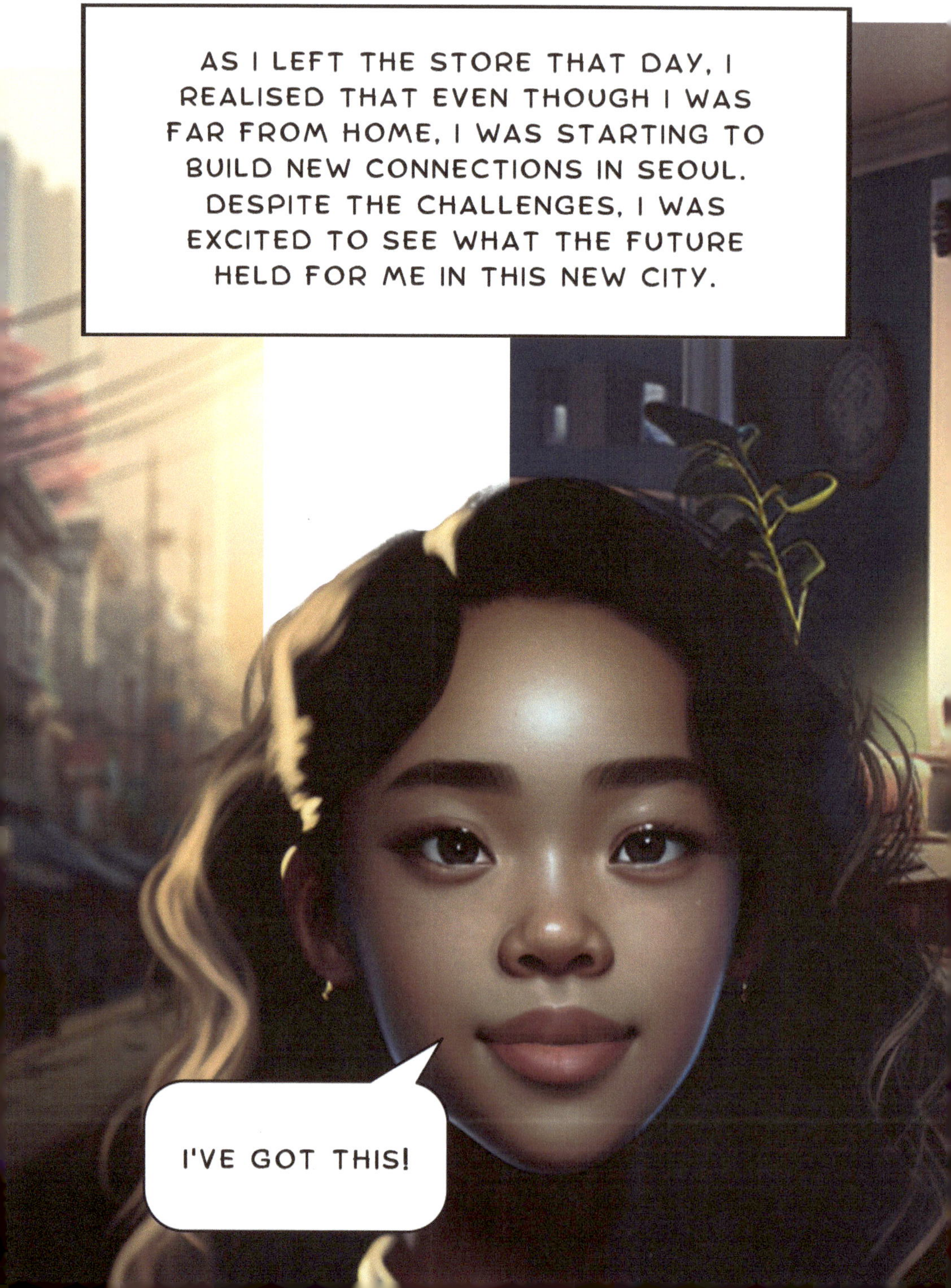

AS I LEFT THE STORE THAT DAY, I REALISED THAT EVEN THOUGH I WAS FAR FROM HOME, I WAS STARTING TO BUILD NEW CONNECTIONS IN SEOUL. DESPITE THE CHALLENGES, I WAS EXCITED TO SEE WHAT THE FUTURE HELD FOR ME IN THIS NEW CITY.

a familiar AURA

CHAPTER 2

2 WEEKS LATER

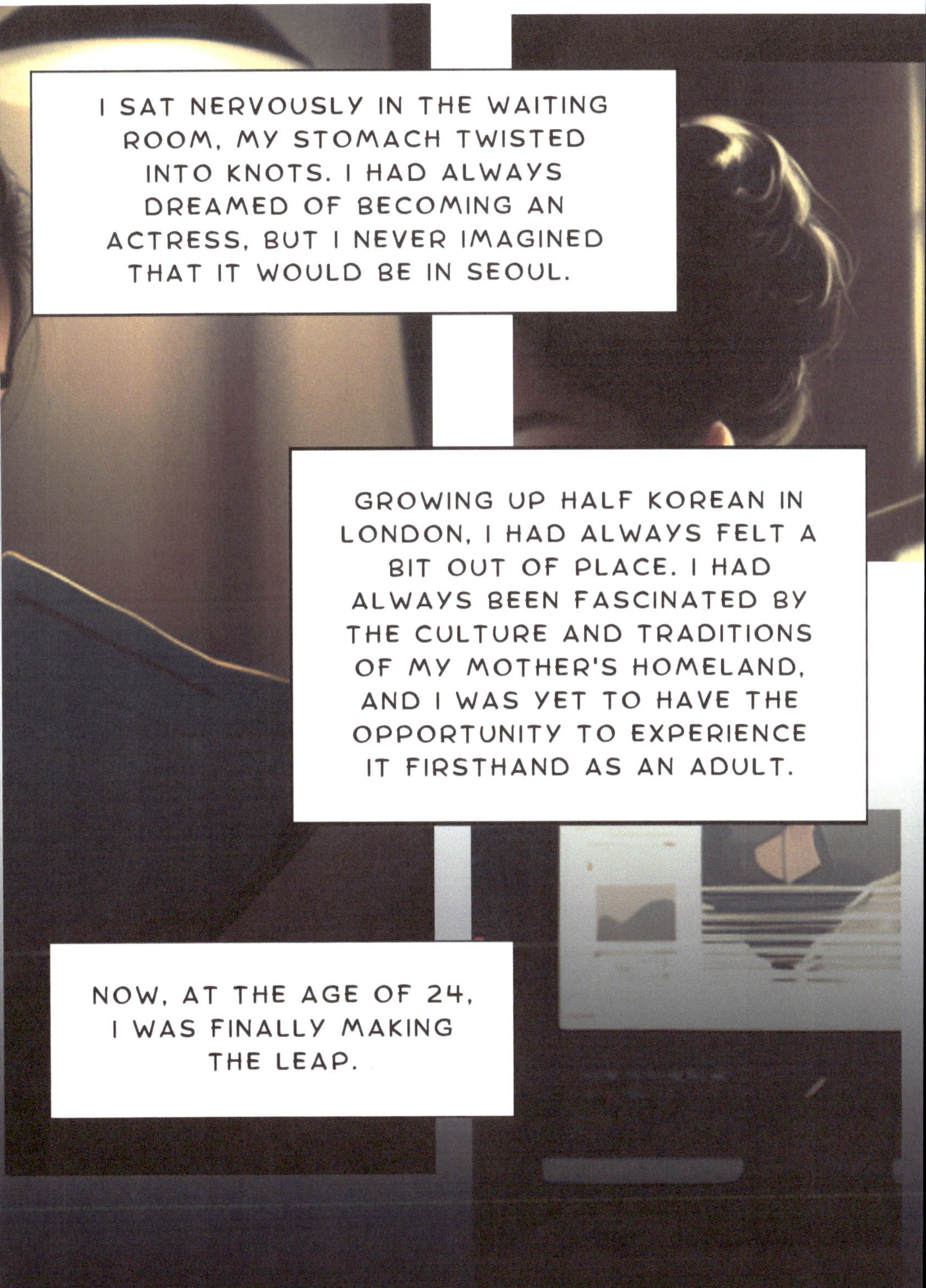

I SAT NERVOUSLY IN THE WAITING ROOM, MY STOMACH TWISTED INTO KNOTS. I HAD ALWAYS DREAMED OF BECOMING AN ACTRESS, BUT I NEVER IMAGINED THAT IT WOULD BE IN SEOUL.

GROWING UP HALF KOREAN IN LONDON, I HAD ALWAYS FELT A BIT OUT OF PLACE. I HAD ALWAYS BEEN FASCINATED BY THE CULTURE AND TRADITIONS OF MY MOTHER'S HOMELAND, AND I WAS YET TO HAVE THE OPPORTUNITY TO EXPERIENCE IT FIRSTHAND AS AN ADULT.

NOW, AT THE AGE OF 24, I WAS FINALLY MAKING THE LEAP.

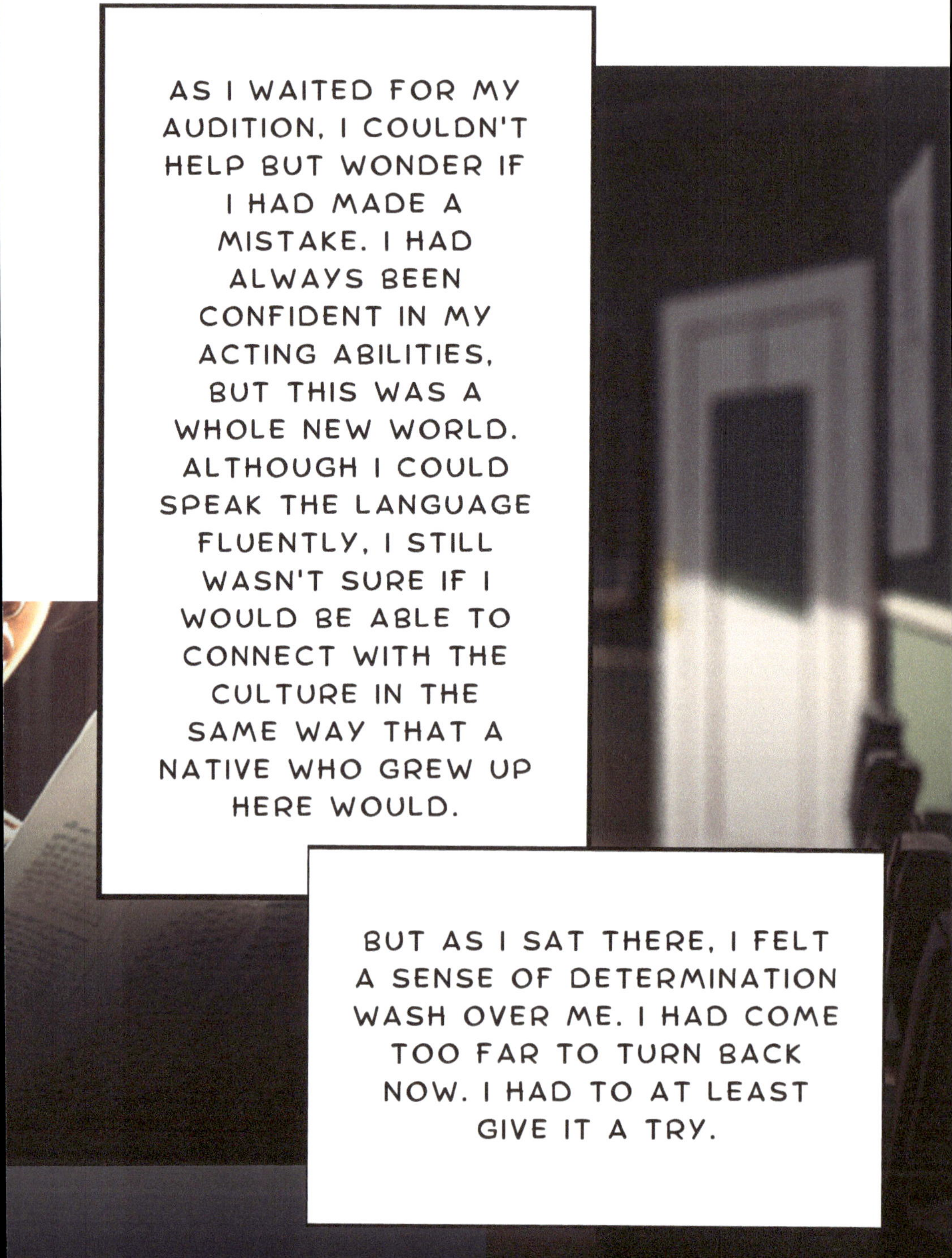

AS I WAITED FOR MY AUDITION, I COULDN'T HELP BUT WONDER IF I HAD MADE A MISTAKE. I HAD ALWAYS BEEN CONFIDENT IN MY ACTING ABILITIES, BUT THIS WAS A WHOLE NEW WORLD. ALTHOUGH I COULD SPEAK THE LANGUAGE FLUENTLY, I STILL WASN'T SURE IF I WOULD BE ABLE TO CONNECT WITH THE CULTURE IN THE SAME WAY THAT A NATIVE WHO GREW UP HERE WOULD.

BUT AS I SAT THERE, I FELT A SENSE OF DETERMINATION WASH OVER ME. I HAD COME TOO FAR TO TURN BACK NOW. I HAD TO AT LEAST GIVE IT A TRY.

FINALLY, MY NAME WAS CALLED AND I STOOD UP, TAKING A DEEP BREATH AS I STEPPED INTO THE AUDITION ROOM. AS I BEGAN TO PERFORM, I FELT A SENSE OF EASE WASH OVER ME. I WAS IN MY ELEMENT, AND I KNEW THAT I WAS GIVING IT MY ALL.

1 HOUR LATER

MAYBE I WASN'T GOOD ENOUGH...

MAYBE I SHOULDN'T HAVE COME...

WE'VE SELECTED YOU FOR THE ROLE...
I COULDN'T BELIEVE MY EARS WHEN THE CASTING DIRECTOR TOLD ME THAT I HAD BEEN CHOSEN FOR THE LEAD ROLE IN 'TANGLED FATES'.
MY DREAM WAS FINALLY COMING TRUE...

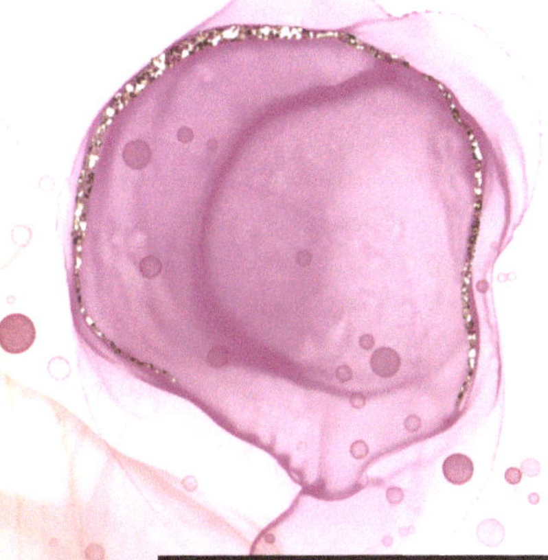

AND TO BE HONEST,
I WAS GENUINELY EXCITED
TO HAVE THE OPPORTUNITY
TO WORK ON A PROJECT
THAT WOULD PUSH ME
OUTSIDE OF MY COMFORT
ZONE. I WAS SO USED TO
WORKING ON ACTION-
THRILLER PROJECTS...

SO, AN ENEMIES TO
LOVERS ROMANCE,
WELL, IT'D DEFINITELY
BE DIFFERENT...

'TANGLED FATES'

- DRAMA SYNOPSIS -

ELITE PROSECUTOR HAN JI-WON (KIM SEO JUN) AND FEARLESS JOURNALIST YOON SE-RI (KIM AALIYAH) ARE SWORN ENEMIES, EACH DRIVEN BY THEIR RELENTLESS PURSUIT OF JUSTICE. WHEN A HIGH-PROFILE CORRUPTION CASE FORCES THEM TO WORK TOGETHER, THEIR CLASHING PERSONALITIES IGNITE A FIERY BATTLE OF WITS AND WILLS.

AS THE INVESTIGATION HEATS UP, A SCANDAL THREATENS TO DESTROY BOTH THEIR CAREERS. TO SAVE FACE AND SALVAGE THE CASE, THEIR FAMILIES ARRANGE A MARRIAGE OF CONVENIENCE,
BINDING THEM IN A CONTRACT FROM WHICH NEITHER CAN ESCAPE. LIVING UNDER ONE ROOF, THEIR CONSTANT FRICTION SLOWLY KINDLES AN UNEXPECTED PASSION.

BUT AS SECRETS UNRAVEL AND DANGER LOOMS, THEIR ENMITY TRANSFORMS INTO AN UNDENIABLE ATTRACTION. IN A WORLD WHERE TRUST IS SCARCE AND EVERY MOVE IS SCRUTINISED, CAN THEY UNTANGLE THEIR FATES, NAVIGATE THE PERILOUS WATERS OF THEIR FAKE MARRIAGE, AND FIND LOVE AMID THE CHAOS? "TANGLED FATES" WEAVES A GRIPPING TALE OF PASSION, BETRAYAL, AND REDEMPTION...

WEEK AFTER WEEK, I THREW MYSELF INTO THE PREPARATION FOR MY ROLE, IMMERSING MYSELF IN THE CULTURE AND TRADITIONS OF KOREA. ALTHOUGH KOREAN CULTURE AND LANGUAGE HAD ALWAYS BEEN A PART OF MY UPBRINGING (THANKS TO MY MOTHER), BEING HERE MADE ME REALISE HOW MUCH MORE I HAD TO LEARN. I WORKED TIRELESSLY TO PERFECT MY ACCENT, FURTHER UNDERSTAND THE NUANCES OF THE LANGUAGE AND EMBRACED ALL OF THE CHALLENGES THAT CAME MY WAY.

FROM STUDYING JOURNALISM TEXTBOOKS TO WATCHING LAW FOCUSED KOREAN DRAMAS, I ABSORBED EVERY ASPECT OF THE PROFESSIONS AND THE CULTURE – MY CULTURE, SAVOURING EACH MORSEL OF UNDERSTANDING.

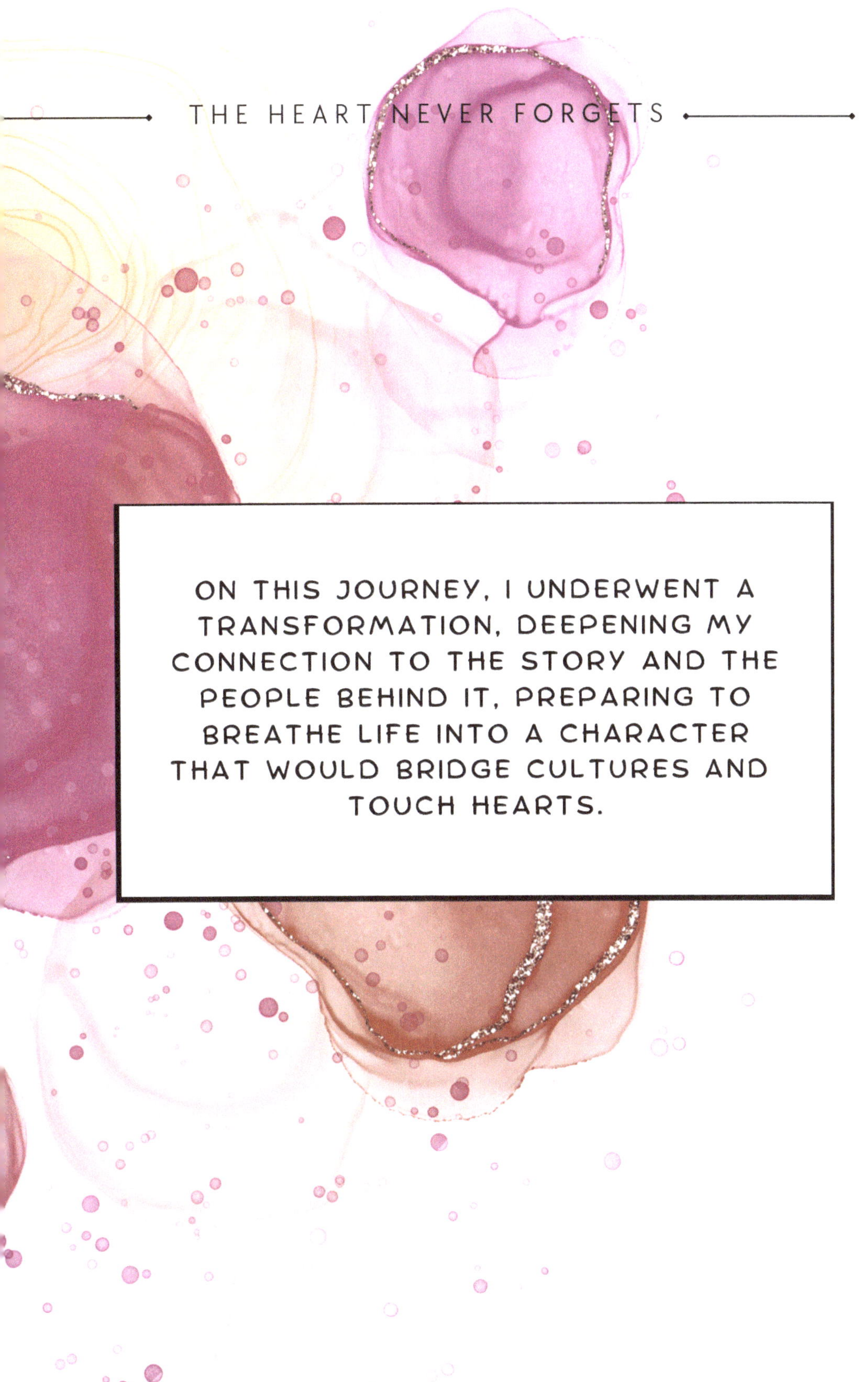

ON THIS JOURNEY, I UNDERWENT A TRANSFORMATION, DEEPENING MY CONNECTION TO THE STORY AND THE PEOPLE BEHIND IT, PREPARING TO BREATHE LIFE INTO A CHARACTER THAT WOULD BRIDGE CULTURES AND TOUCH HEARTS.

THE HEART NEVER FORGETS
BUT...

FROM TIME TO TIME,
I COULD SENSE

THE PIERCING STARES AND JUDGMENTAL GLANCES FROM THE OTHER CAST AND CREW MEMBERS. THEIR WHISPERED REMARKS ABOUT ME NOT BEING "TRULY" KOREAN AND NOT DESERVING OF MY ROLE ECHOED IN MY MIND, CASTING DOUBT ON MY IDENTITY AND BELONGING.

CAUGHT BETWEEN TWO WORLDS, I OFTEN FELT LIKE I WAS TOO KOREAN FOR THE WEST AND TOO WESTERN FOR KOREA. THEIR COMMENTS USED TO BRING ME DOWN, MAKING ME QUESTION MY PLACE IN THIS INDUSTRY AND MY WORTH AS AN ARTIST. BUT ONE DAY, WHEN I LEAST EXPECTED IT, THE DIRECTOR PULLED ME ASIDE, HIS EYES FILLED WITH UNDERSTANDING, AND SPOKE WORDS THAT WOULD FOREVER CHANGE MY PERSPECTIVE…

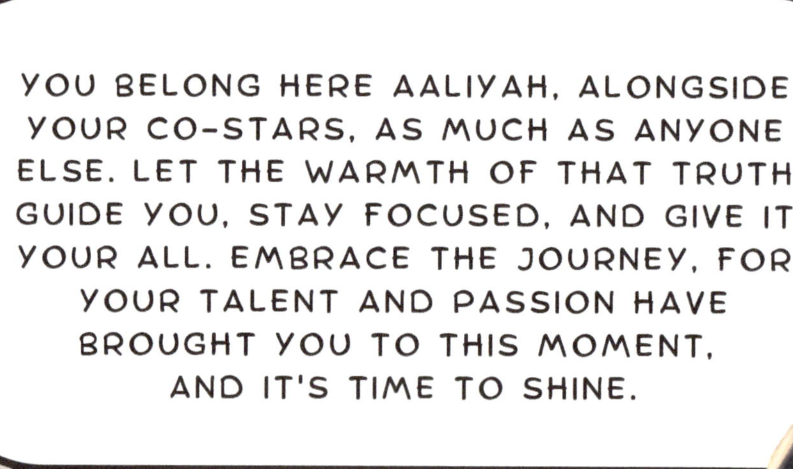
YOU BELONG HERE AALIYAH, ALONGSIDE YOUR CO-STARS, AS MUCH AS ANYONE ELSE. LET THE WARMTH OF THAT TRUTH GUIDE YOU, STAY FOCUSED, AND GIVE IT YOUR ALL. EMBRACE THE JOURNEY, FOR YOUR TALENT AND PASSION HAVE BROUGHT YOU TO THIS MOMENT, AND IT'S TIME TO SHINE.

a familiar AURA

2 WEEK LATER

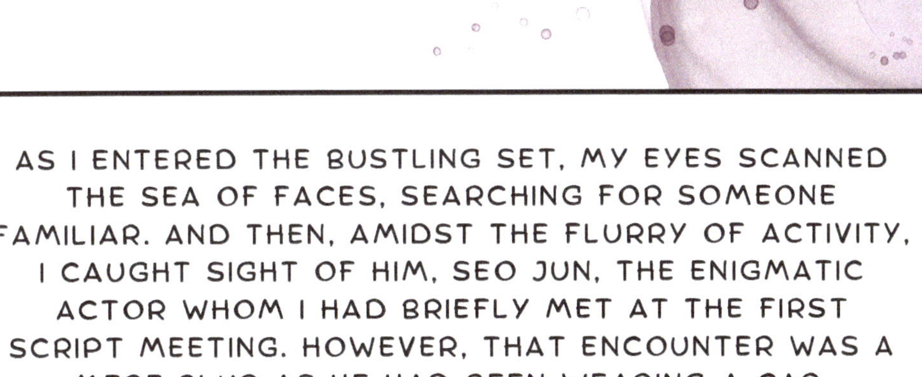

AS I ENTERED THE BUSTLING SET, MY EYES SCANNED THE SEA OF FACES, SEARCHING FOR SOMEONE FAMILIAR. AND THEN, AMIDST THE FLURRY OF ACTIVITY, I CAUGHT SIGHT OF HIM, SEO JUN, THE ENIGMATIC ACTOR WHOM I HAD BRIEFLY MET AT THE FIRST SCRIPT MEETING. HOWEVER, THAT ENCOUNTER WAS A MERE BLUR AS HE HAD BEEN WEARING A CAP, OBSCURING HIS FEATURES.

CHAPTER 3

NOW, SEEING HIM WITHOUT ANY BARRIERS, MY BREATH HITCHED IN MY THROAT. SEO JUN STOOD TALL AT 6'1, HIS DARK, LUSTROUS HAIR FRAMING A FACE THAT SEEMED CARVED BY THE HANDS OF AN ARTIST. HIS BROAD SHOULDERS AND COMMANDING PRESENCE EXUDED AN AIR OF CONFIDENCE, MAKING HIM THE EPITOME OF A POWERFUL AND REPUTABLE MALE LEAD. IN THE DIMLY LIT ROOM, HIS PRESENCE COMMANDED ATTENTION WITH EVERY STEP. HE POSSESSED A MAGNETIC ALLURE, A BEGUILING BLEND OF RUGGED CHARM AND REFINED ELEGANCE THAT LEFT BOTH MEN AND WOMEN SPELLBOUND.

INTIMIDATION CREPT OVER ME, MY NERVES FLUTTERING LIKE A TRAPPED BIRD IN MY CHEST. HOW COULD I, A RELATIVELY UNKNOWN ACTRESS, STAND ALONGSIDE SOMEONE AS CAPTIVATING AS SEO JUN? THE WEIGHT OF HIS REPUTATION AND THE EXPECTATIONS SURROUNDING HIM SEEMED TO PRESS DOWN UPON MY SHOULDERS, AMPLIFYING MY ANXIETY.

AS I OBSERVED HIM FROM AFAR, A MIX OF AWE AND APPREHENSION SWIRLED WITHIN ME. HIS GORGEOUS EYES HELD A DEPTH THAT I YEARNED TO EXPLORE, YET THEY ALSO HARBOURED AN INTENSITY THAT SENT SHIVERS DOWN MY SPINE. IT WAS AS IF HE CARRIED THE WEIGHT OF THE WORLD IN THOSE EYES, A WEIGHT THAT I FEARED WOULD CRUSH ME UNDER ITS GAZE.

BRIEFLY, OUR EYES MET, AND A FLEETING CONNECTION SPARKED BETWEEN US. IN THAT MOMENT, I GLIMPSED A GLIMMER OF CURIOSITY IN HIS EXPRESSION—A HINT OF RECOGNITION, PERHAPS. BUT IT VANISHED AS QUICKLY AS IT HAD APPEARED, LEAVING ME TO WONDER IF IT WAS A FIGMENT OF MY IMAGINATION.

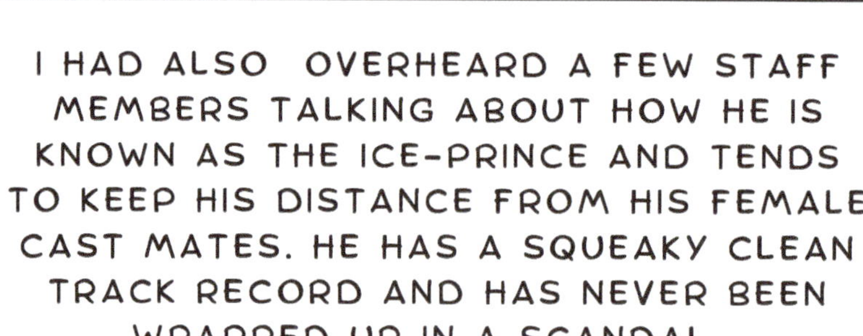

AS WORK WENT ON WITH THE DRAMA, I FOUND MYSELF BUTTING HEADS SEO JUN.

I HAD ALSO OVERHEARD A FEW STAFF MEMBERS TALKING ABOUT HOW HE IS KNOWN AS THE ICE-PRINCE AND TENDS TO KEEP HIS DISTANCE FROM HIS FEMALE CAST MATES. HE HAS A SQUEAKY CLEAN TRACK RECORD AND HAS NEVER BEEN WRAPPED UP IN A SCANDAL...

COULD THAT BE WHY HE SEEMS SO COLD?

HE SEEMED TO BE ANNOYED WITH ME FROM THE START, AND I COULDN'T UNDERSTAND WHY. I HAD ALWAYS BEEN PROFESSIONAL ON SET, AND I COULDN'T UNDERSTAND WHY HE SEEMED TO HAVE SUCH A PROBLEM WITH ME...
WAS WAS IT BECAUSE OF THE FACT THAT I WAS A LESSER KNOWN ACTOR IN KOREA, DID HE DOUBT MY CAPABILITIES OF DOING A GOOD JOB?

3 WEEK LATER

THE DAY THINGS CHANGED...

MY HEART RACED AS I PACED BACK AND FORTH IN MY TRAILER

THE WEIGHT OF THE UPCOMING SCENE HEAVY ON MY MIND. THE UNDENIABLE TENSION BETWEEN SEO JUN AND I HAD GROWN WITH EACH PASSING DAY...

ALTHOUGH HE HAD APPEARED DISTANT AND COLD TOWARDS ME, I COULDN'T IGNORE THE MAGNETIC PULL THAT DREW ME CLOSER TO HIM- WAS IT ADMIRATION FOR A COLLEAGUE AND THE DEEP DESIRE TO DO WELL OR SOMETHING ELSE?..

KNOCK

KNOCK

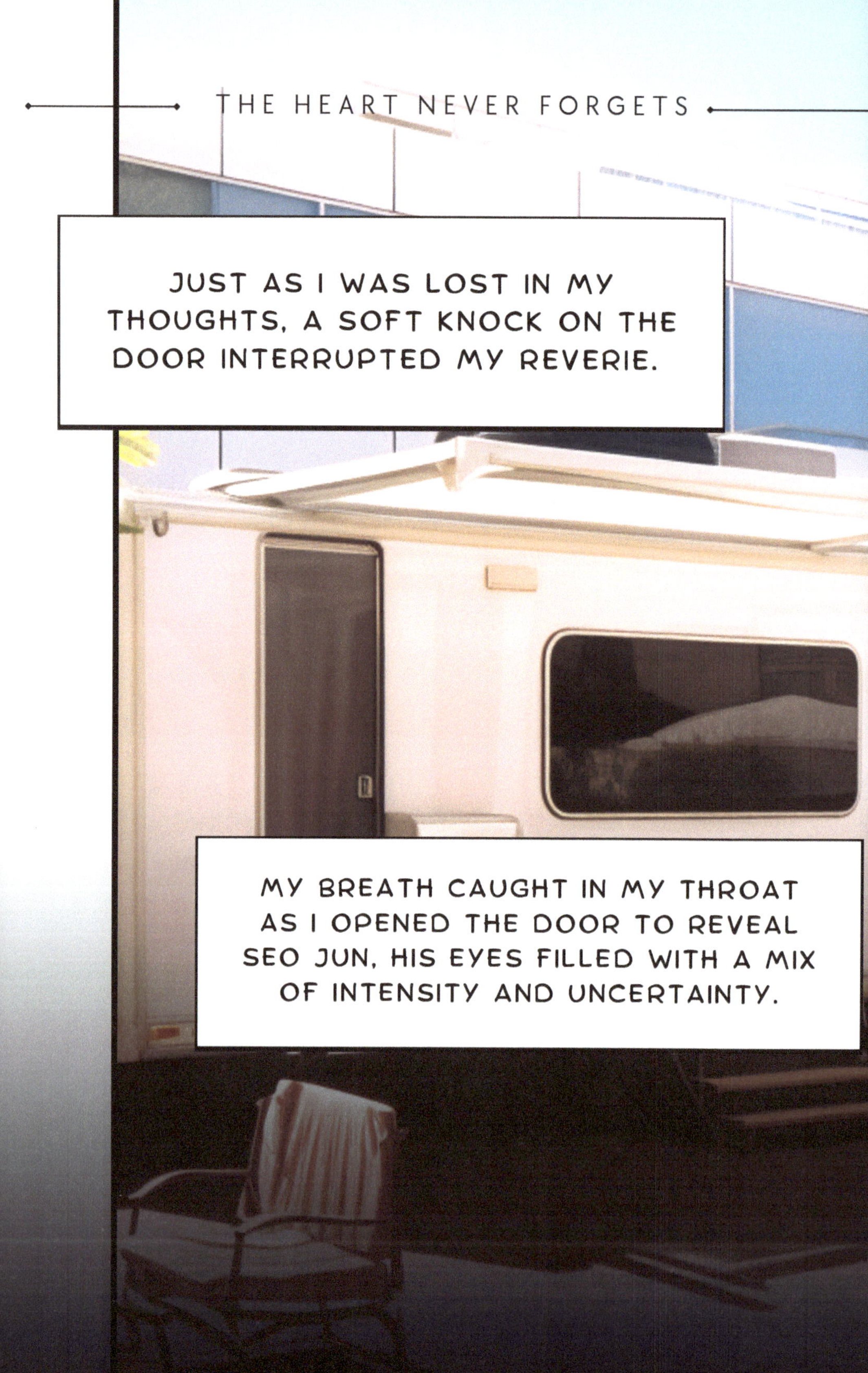
THE HEART NEVER FORGETS

JUST AS I WAS LOST IN MY THOUGHTS, A SOFT KNOCK ON THE DOOR INTERRUPTED MY REVERIE.

MY BREATH CAUGHT IN MY THROAT AS I OPENED THE DOOR TO REVEAL SEO JUN, HIS EYES FILLED WITH A MIX OF INTENSITY AND UNCERTAINTY.

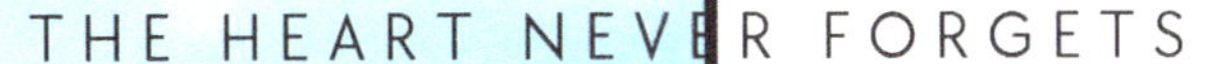

HEY, AALIYAH. MIND IF I COME IN?
I THOUGHT WE COULD PRACTISE OUR LINES BEFORE FILMING THE SCENE

SEO JUN STEPPED INSIDE, AND THE ROOM SEEMED TO SHRINK IN THE PRESENCE OF OUR UNSPOKEN TENSION.

SEO JUN EXPLAINED

SEATED ON THE EDGE OF THE SOFA, OUR SCRIPTS HELD TIGHTLY IN OUR HANDS, I COULD FEEL THE ENERGY IN THE AIR, CRACKLING WITH ANTICIPATION.

ALRIGHT, LET'S BEGIN. I'LL START WITH MY LINES,

HE BEGAN RECITING HIS LINES, HIS VOICE CARRYING A NUANCED BLEND OF INDIFFERENCE AND HIDDEN LONGING. I MIRRORED HIS PERFORMANCE, MY VOICE CAREFULLY MODULATED TO CONVEY THE DELICATE BALANCE OF DESIRE AND RESTRAINT REQUIRED FOR THE SCENE.

AS WE REHEARSED, MY TREMBLING HAND REACHED OUT TO TOUCH SEO JUN'S CHEST, AS PER THE STAGE DIRECTIONS. TO MY SURPRISE, I COULD FEEL HIS HEART POUNDING BENEATH MY PALM, A RHYTHM THAT QUITE MATCHED MY OWN.

THE TENSION IN THE ROOM PAIRED WITH THE LACK OF BREAKFAST I CHOSE TO HAVE THAT MORNING WAS DEFINITELY A TERRIBLE IDEA AND TO MY DISMAY MY STOMACH LET OUT A LOUD GRUMBLE...

IN RESPONSE, SEO JUN LET OUT A SOFT CHUCKLE, HIS LAUGHTER FILLED WITH A HINT OF VULNERABILITY, ECHOING THROUGH THE ROOM LIKE A BITTERSWEET MELODY.

SOMEONE'S UPSET – IT SEEMS THAT I'M NOT THE ONLY ONE WHO CHOSE TO SKIP BREAKFAST TODAY,

SEO JUN REMARKED

HE REACHED INTO HIS POCKET AND HANDED ME A SLIGHTLY DISFIGURED AND WARM SAMGAK KIMBAB.
EMBARRASSED, I BLUSHED, FEELING MY CHEEKS WARM.
I, I APOLOGISE. MY STOMACH SEEMS TO HAVE A MIND OF ITS OWN...
STAMMER
STAMMER

SEO JUN'S SMILE WIDENED, HIS EYES CRINKLING AT THE CORNERS.

DON'T WORRY ABOUT IT. IT'S ENDEARING, REALLY...

REASURING - REASURING

REASURING

AS WE CONTINUED TO PRACTISE, OUR CHEMISTRY DEEPENED, OUR WORDS FLOWING EFFORTLESSLY, AS THOUGH OUR SOULS HAD FOUND A COMMON RHYTHM.

I COULDN'T HELP BUT BE DRAWN FURTHER INTO SEO JUN'S ENIGMATIC PRESENCE.

AS WE CONTINUED TO RECITE OUR LINES...

FOLLOWING THE STAGE DIRECTIONS, SEO JUN HELD MY WAIST WITH THIS LEFT ARM AND THEN BEGAN TO MOVE HIS RIGHT HAND CLOSER TO MY CHEST...

FIRST STOPPING JUST OVER MY HEART – HE LAID HIS HAND DOWN GENTLY AND I FELT MY WHOLE BODY TENSE UP AND IN TURN, REVEALING HOW NERVOUS I TRULY WAS IN THIS UNFATHOMABLE SITUATION...

HIS HAND THEN GRADUALLY NAVIGATED FROM MY HEART TO THE CENTRE OF MY CHEST, HIS FINGERS DELICATELY TRACED THE OUTLINE OF MY COLLARBONES, THE BACK OF MY NECK AND THEN SLOWLY, HE BRUSHED OVER MY LIPS WITH HIS THUMB. IN ANY OTHER SITUATION, SOMEONE DOING SUCH A THING WOULD ABSOLUTELY REPULSE ME BUT THIS WAS DIFFERENT.

I FELT A SURGE OF ELECTRICITY, DESIRE AND TREPIDATION FILL MY SYSTEM. IT WAS AS IF HE WAS UNRAVELLING THE DEPTHS OF MY BEING, MAPPING MY VULNERABILITIES, AND EXPLORING MY DEEPEST LONGINGS.

I TRIED TO STEADY MY BREATHING, TO REGAIN CONTROL OVER THE WHIRLWIND OF EMOTIONS INSIDE ME.

I THOUGHT TO MYSELF,

IN HOPES THAT THE

REALISATION WOULD
HELP ME REGAIN MY
COMPOSURE…

IN THAT MOMENT, SEO JUN LEANED IN, OUR FACES MERE INCHES APART,

OUR EYES LOCKED IN A PASSIONATE GAZE. TIME SEEMED TO STAND STILL AS WE EMBRACED OUR ROLES,

OUR LIPS MEETING IN A BREATHTAKING UNION...

IN THAT STOLEN MOMENT,..

THE WORLD AROUND US FADED INTO INSIGNIFICANCE. THE SCENE TRANSFORMED FROM A MERE ACT OF SCRIPTED PASSION INTO A TESTAMENT TO THE RAW POWER OF UNION AND DESIRE. OUR BODIES HUMMED WITH ELECTRIC ENERGY, OUR CONNECTION RESONATING WITH A DEPTH THAT SURPASSED THE LIMITATIONS OF THE SILVER SCREEN.

AS WE FINALLY BROKE OUR KISS, OUR EYES REMAINED LOCKED, REVEALING A COMPLEX TAPESTRY OF EMOTIONS. I SAW NOT ONLY THE HIDDEN DESIRES AND VULNERABILITY IN SEO JUN'S GAZE BUT ALSO A REFLECTION OF MY OWN FEARS AND LONGING. IN THAT PROFOUND EXCHANGE, WE HAD TRANSCENDED OUR ROLES AS ACTORS, BECOMING TWO SOULS YEARNING FOR AN AUTHENTIC CONNECTION AMIDST THE CHAOS OF OUR ONSCREEN PERSONAS.

AS THE LINGERING INTENSITY OF OUR INTIMATE MOMENT BEGAN TO SETTLE,...

KNOCK

A SUDDEN KNOCK AT THE DOOR SHATTERED THE FRAGILE BUBBLE WE HAD CREATED.

STARTLED, I LOOKED TOWARDS THE ENTRANCE, PANIC FLUTTERING IN MY CHEST. SEO JUN, TOO, SEEMED TAKEN ABACK, HIS EYES FILLED WITH A MIX OF REGRET AND APPREHENSION.

SEO JUN MUTTERED, HIS VOICE LACED WITH A HINT OF DISAPPOINTMENT.

RELUCTANTLY, HE MADE HIS WAY TOWARDS THE DOOR, STEALING ONE LAST GLANCE IN MY DIRECTION. IN THAT FLEETING MOMENT, I COULDN'T DECIPHER THE EMOTIONS FLICKERING ACROSS HIS FACE. DID HE FEEL THE SAME CONNECTION I DID, OR WAS IT MERELY THE FACADE OF A SKILLED ACTOR?

AS SEO JUN STEPPED OUT OF THE TRAILER, MY MANAGER ENTERED, HIS PRESENCE JOLTING ME BACK TO REALITY. HE WORE A KNOWING SMILE, HIS EYES SCANNING THE ROOM FOR ANY SIGNS OF IMPROPRIETY. I COULD FEEL THE WEIGHT OF HIS EXPECTATIONS, THE UNSPOKEN DEMAND FOR PROFESSIONALISM HANGING HEAVILY IN THE AIR.

EVERYTHING GOING ALRIGHT, AALIYAH?

HE ASKED, HIS TONE LACED WITH A MIXTURE OF CONCERN AND SUSPICION.

HE = AALIYAH'S MANAGER

HE ONLY CALLS ME AALIYAH WHEN HE'S IN A SERIOUS MOOD...

THOSE CLOSE TO AALIYAH CALL HER LIYAH

UNEASY

UNEASY

I NODDED, TRYING TO REGAIN MY COMPOSURE.

YES, EVERYTHING'S FINE, WAS JUST GOING THROUGH THE SCENE WITH SEO JUN...

WITH A RAISED EYEBROW, MY MANAGER SHOT ME A KNOWING LOOK.

ALRIGHT THEN. REMEMBER, PROFESSIONALISM COMES FIRST.

WE'RE HERE TO MAKE A SUCCESSFUL DRAMA, NOT TO INDULGE IN PERSONAL FANTASIES OR WORSE, START A SCANDAL.

IN THAT MOMENT,..

HIS WORDS STUNG, A REMINDER OF THE DELICATE LINE I WAS TREADING BETWEEN FICTION AND REALITY. I NODDED ONCE AGAIN, SILENTLY ACKNOWLEDGING HIS ADMONITION.

2 HOURS LATER

ON THE SET, THE ATMOSPHERE BUZZED WITH ANTICIPATION AS THE CREW PREPARED FOR THE FILMING OF THE SCENE. THE DIRECTOR GATHERED US TOGETHER, HIS VOICE RESONATING WITH A MIXTURE OF EXCITEMENT AND AUTHORITY.

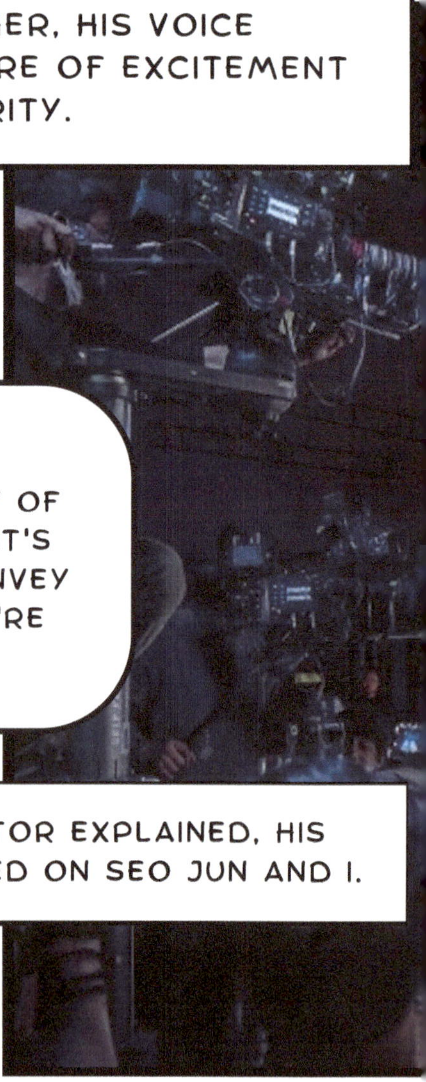

TODAY, WE'RE GOING TO CAPTURE THE RAW INTENSITY OF THIS PASSIONATE MOMENT. IT'S CRUCIAL THAT YOU BOTH CONVEY THE DEPTH OF EMOTION WE'RE AIMING FOR...

THE DIRECTOR EXPLAINED, HIS EYES FOCUSED ON SEO JUN AND I.

I EXCHANGED A NERVOUS GLANCE WITH SEO JUN, FEELING A MIXTURE OF EXCITEMENT AND TREPIDATION. THIS SCENE HELD THE POTENTIAL TO DEEPEN OUR CHARACTERS' CONNECTION OR SHATTER THE FRAGILE ILLUSION WE HAD CREATED.

AS THE DIRECTOR CALLED FOR ACTION, WE STEPPED INTO OUR CHARACTERS' SKINS, OUR BODIES MOVING WITH A HEIGHTENED AWARENESS OF EACH OTHER. THE AIR CRACKLED WITH ANTICIPATION AS OUR LIPS DREW CLOSER, THE WEIGHT OF OUR PREVIOUS ENCOUNTER LINGERING IN THE AIR.

HOWEVER, SEO JUN'S PERFORMANCE SEEMED SLIGHTLY OFF, HIS LINES FALTERING AND HIS MOVEMENTS LACKING THE USUAL PRECISION. EACH TIME HE STUMBLED, WE HAD TO REDO THE SCENE, AMPLIFYING THE INTENSITY OF OUR ONSCREEN CONNECTION. WITH EACH TAKE, DOUBT CREPT INTO MY MIND....

FRUSTRATION ETCHED ACROSS THE DIRECTOR'S FACE AS WE WENT THROUGH MULTIPLE RETAKES. HE CALLED FOR A MOMENTARY PAUSE, HIS GAZE FOCUSED ON SEO JUN.
SEO JUN, WE NEED YOU TO BE MORE FOCUSED. THESE MISTAKES ARE SLOWING DOWN THE ENTIRE PRODUCTION,
THE DIRECTOR REPRIMANDED

SEO JUN'S SHOULDERS SLUMPED SLIGHTLY, HIS EYES FILLED WITH AN INNOCENT, SHEEPISH GRIN.

I APOLOGISE, DIRECTOR. IT WON'T HAPPEN AGAIN.

AS WE RESUMED FILMING, I COULDN'T HELP BUT WONDER IF THERE WAS MORE TO SEO JUN'S REPEATED SLIP-UPS. THE WAY HIS EYES CRINKLED AT THE CORNERS, THE SUBTLE CURVE OF HIS LIPS—IT ALL HINTED AT A MISCHIEVOUS INTENTION. DID HE WANT MORE INTIMATE MOMENTS WITH ME, OR WAS IT MY IMAGINATION PLAYING TRICKS ON ME?

IN THAT TUMULTUOUS SEA OF UNCERTAINTY, WE CONTINUED TO NAVIGATE THE SCENE, OUR PERFORMANCES INTERTWINING IN A DELICATE DANCE OF DESIRE AND RESTRAINT. THE DIRECTOR'S EXPECTATIONS WEIGHED HEAVILY UPON ME, AND I STRIVED TO DELIVER MY BEST, EVEN AMIDST THE LINGERING DOUBTS AND UNANSWERED QUESTIONS.

WITH EACH TAKE, SEO JUN'S PERFORMANCE GREW MORE REFINED, HIS LINES DELIVERED WITH PRECISION AND HIS MOVEMENTS EXUDING THE DESIRED PASSION. THE CHEMISTRY BETWEEN US INTENSIFIED, AND IT BECAME INCREASINGLY DIFFICULT TO SEPARATE THE SCENE FROM REALITY.

AS THE DIRECTOR CALLED FOR ANOTHER TAKE,

SEO JUN PULLED ME IN, HIS WARM BREATH ON MY NECK AND WHISPERED...
LET'S DO IT LIKE WE DID EARLIER...
WHISPER
WHISPER
WHISPER
JUST LIKE HOW...
WE DID "IT" IN YOUR TRAILER

GASP

GASP

I WASN'T SURE IF IT WAS BECAUSE OF THE BOLD WAY IN WHICH HE STRUCTURED THE STATEMENT OR THE FACT THAT I WAS CAUGHT OFF GUARD AND COULD FEEL HIS WARM BREATH ON MY EAR IN SUCH AN EXPOSED ENVIRONMENT BUT WHATEVER THE CASE, MY KNEES BEGAN TO FEEL WEAK AND MY MIND WENT BLANK FOR A MOMENT...

NEVERTHELESS I DID MY BEST TO GATHER MYSELF...

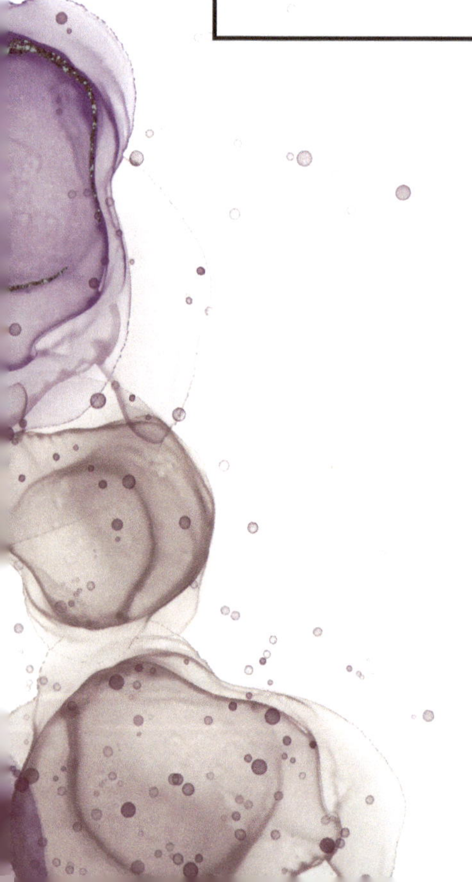

AS WE PROCEEDED WITH SHOOTING, I FOUND MYSELF CAUGHT IN SEO JUN'S GAZE. HIS EYES HELD A FLICKER OF SOMETHING BEYOND THE SCRIPT—A HINT OF LONGING, PERHAPS, OR AN UNSPOKEN DESIRE. IT WAS IN THOSE FLEETING MOMENTS, AMIDST THE CHAOS OF SET, THAT I ALLOWED MYSELF TO BELIEVE THAT THERE MIGHT BE MORE TO OUR ONSCREEN ROMANCE.

THE DIRECTOR'S VOICE ECHOED IN THE BACKGROUND, HIS INSTRUCTIONS PUNCTUATED BY THE HUM OF THE CAMERAS AND THE HUSHED WHISPERS OF THE CREW. HE EMPHASISED THE NEED FOR AUTHENTICITY, URGING US TO DIVE DEEPER INTO OUR CHARACTERS' SOULS AND LET THE SPARKS BETWEEN US IGNITE THE SCENE.

TIME SEEMED TO STRETCH AS WE APPROACHED THE PIVOTAL MOMENT—THE ANTICIPATED KISS THAT WOULD ENCAPSULATE THE SIMMERING TENSION BETWEEN OUR CHARACTERS. THE AIR CRACKLED WITH ELECTRICITY, AND I COULD FEEL THE WEIGHT OF SEO JUN'S GAZE, HIS PRESENCE BOTH COMFORTING AND UNNERVING...

AS OUR LIPS MET, THE WORLD AROUND US FADED INTO INSIGNIFICANCE. THE TOUCH WAS FLEETING YET SEARING, A DELICATE DANCE OF VULNERABILITY AND DESIRE. IN THAT MOMENT, I ALLOWED MYSELF TO SUCCUMB TO THE WHIRLWIND OF EMOTIONS, LOSING MYSELF IN THE INTRICACIES OF OUR CHARACTERS' LOVE...

THE DIRECTOR CALLED FOR ANOTHER TAKE, SEEKING PERFECTION IN EVERY NUANCED DETAIL. WE OBLIGED, THE PASSION AND YEARNING DEEPENING WITH EACH REPETITION. TIME BLURRED AS WE SURRENDERED TO THE EBB AND FLOW OF THE SCENE, EXPLORING THE UNSPOKEN DESIRES AND UNCHARTED TERRITORIES OF OUR CHARACTERS' HEARTS.

AS THE FINAL TAKE CONCLUDED, A HUSHED SILENCE ENVELOPED THE SET. THE DIRECTOR, WEARING A SUBTLE SMILE OF SATISFACTION, COMMENDED OUR PERFORMANCES. WE HAD MANAGED TO CAPTURE THE ESSENCE OF A LOVE THAT DEFIED LOGIC AND IGNITED THE SCREEN WITH ITS INTENSITY.

SEO JUN AND I EXCHANGED A KNOWING GLANCE, OUR EYES MIRRORING THE UNSPOKEN CONNECTION THAT HAD GROWN BETWEEN US. WHETHER IT WAS A RESULT OF OUR SHARED EXPERIENCES OR SIMPLY THE MAGIC OF THE STAGE, WE COULDN'T DENY THE PALPABLE CHEMISTRY THAT INFUSED OUR PERFORMANCES.

AS WE STEPPED AWAY FROM THE SET, THE ECHOES OF OUR CHARACTERS' LOVE LINGERED IN THE AIR, INTERTWINING WITH THE UNSPOKEN QUESTIONS AND UNDENIABLE ATTRACTION THAT HAD EMERGED BETWEEN US.

THE BOUNDARIES BETWEEN FICTION AND REALITY HAD BECOME BLURRED, AND I COULDN'T HELP BUT WONDER WHAT LAY AHEAD FOR SEO JUN AND ME—BOTH ONSCREEN AND OFF.

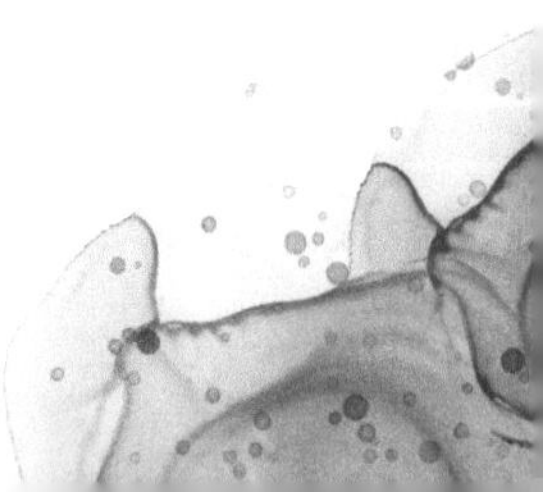

AURA

CHAPTER 4

2 WEEK LATER

AS THE WEEKS WENT BY, I BEGAN TO SEE A DIFFERENT SIDE OF SEO JUN. HE WAS FIERCELY DEDICATED TO HIS CRAFT, AND HE SEEMED TO HAVE A GENUINE PASSION FOR ACTING.
I REALISED THAT HIS INITIAL COLDNESS TOWARDS ME WAS ACTUALLY SHYNESS AND AS WE SPENT MORE AND MORE TIME TOGETHER, HE REALLY TRIED HIS BEST TO MAKE SURE THAT I ALWAYS FELT COMFORTABLE AND SUPPORTED...
LIYAH, DO YOU NEED ANY HELP, TODAYS SCRIPT IS A BIT MORE DIFFICULT DUE TO THE POLITICAL TERMINOLOGY?
*LIYAH: IS AALIYAH'S NICKNAME

AS TIME WENT ON, WE BEGAN TO BOND OVER OUR COMMON INTERESTS; TRAVEL, READING AND RANDOM GUILTY PLEASURES LIKE ASMR COOKING CHANNELS AND ANIMATED FILMS. OUR COMING TOGETHER FELT SO ORGANIC, WE EVEN STARTED TO HANG OUT OUTSIDE OF FILMING, WHICH WAS DIFFICULT AT TIMES DUE TO HIS FANS... AND ME NOT WANTING TO GET WRAPPED UP IN A SCANDAL ESPECIALLY SO EARLY ON IN MY CAREER...

BUT WE MADE THINGS WORK AND AS WE BOTH BECAME MORE COMFORTABLE AROUND ONE ANOTHER, WE BEGAN TO OPEN UP TO ONE ANOTHER ABOUT OUR DREAMS, GOALS AND CHILDHOODS...

HE WOULD ALWAYS SAY THAT HE ADMIRED MY PASSION, CREATIVITY AND PERSEVERANCE DESPITE MY ADVERSITY, AND I APPRECIATED HEARING SUCH WARM WORDS FROM HIM... THEY MADE ME FEEL AT PEACE FOR SOME REASON...

HIS ENCOURAGEMENT
BEGAN TO MEAN SO
MUCH TO ME...

THE MORE TIME WE SPENT TOGETHER AND INTERACTING, THE MORE I FOUND MYSELF LONGING FOR HIS COMPANY, COUNTING DOWN TO THE NEXT TIME WE'D BE ABLE TO SPEND TIME TOGETHER...

WAS I STARTING TO FALL FOR HIM?

FROM TIME TO TIME I FIND MY MIND WONDERING ...THINKING ABOUT WHAT LIFE WOULD LOOK LIKE IF WE BECAME MORE...

MORE THAN JUST FRIENDLY ACQUAINTANCES...

WHAT IF WE BECAME

SOMETHING MORE...

1 WEEK LATER

SEO JUN (SUNBAE)

LIYAH DO YOU HAVE
SCHEDULE TODAY?

11:00 AM

HI~ I'M FREE
AFTER 1PM

11:05 AM

SEO JUN (SUNBAE)

COFFEE MEET AT 2PM
~ I'LL PICK YOU UP?

11:06 AM

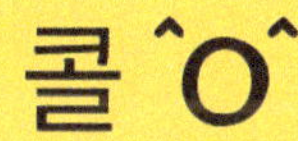

11:10 AM

KNOCK
KNOCK

OPPA YOU'RE HERE...
LIYAH, I WAS SO NERVOUS AND I'VE BEEN WALKING UP AND DOWN OUTSIDE YOUR APARTMENT FOR AN HOUR...
I WANTED TO TELL YOU THAT...
WHAT IS HAPPENING RIGHT NOW?

YOU ARE "MY PERSON" LIYAH...

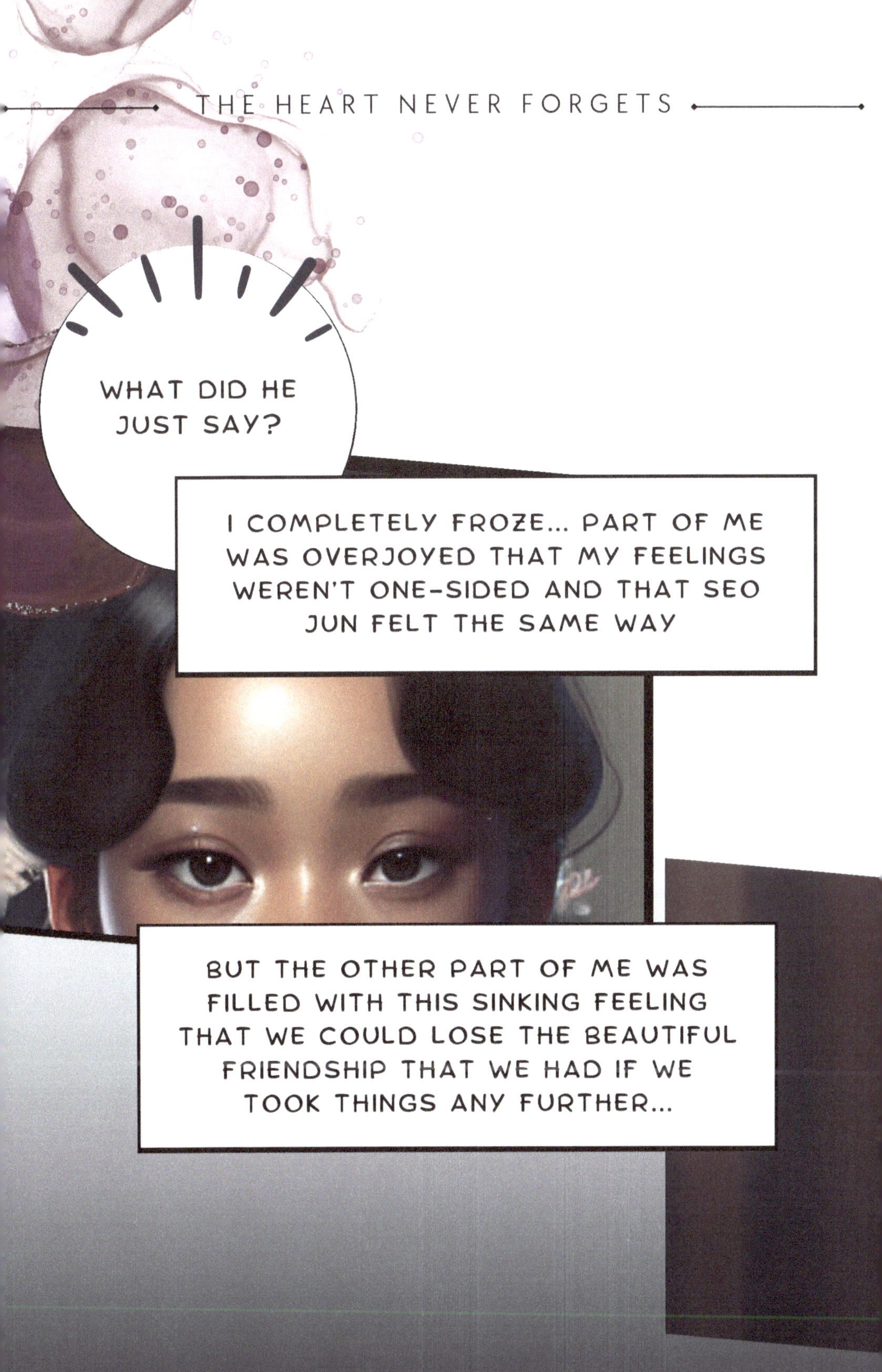
WHAT DID HE
JUST SAY?

I COMPLETELY FROZE... PART OF ME
WAS OVERJOYED THAT MY FEELINGS
WEREN'T ONE-SIDED AND THAT SEO
JUN FELT THE SAME WAY

BUT THE OTHER PART OF ME WAS
FILLED WITH THIS SINKING FEELING
THAT WE COULD LOSE THE BEAUTIFUL
FRIENDSHIP THAT WE HAD IF WE
TOOK THINGS ANY FURTHER...

BUZZZ

BUZZZ

MANAGERNIM

LIYAH DID YOU EAT TODAY?

10:00 AM

10:02 AM

MANAGERNIM

LIYAH!!! KETFLIX HAVE CASTED YOU IN A NEW PROJECT. YOU DONE IT! WE FLY TO LONDON TO FILM RIGHT AFTER YOU WRAP SHOOTING ON THE DRAMA.

6:36 PM

MANAGERNIM

CAN I CONFIRM THAT YOU ARE STILL HAPPY TO TAKE THE PROJECT?

6:38 PM

I COMPLETELY FROZE... PART OF ME WAS OVERJOYED THAT MY FEELINGS WEREN'T ONE-SIDED AND THAT SEO JUN FELT THE SAME WAY

I FOUND MYSELF FACED WITH A DIFFICULT DECISION. I HAD ALWAYS DREAMED OF BECOMING AN ACTRESS, BUT I HAD NEVER IMAGINED THAT IT WOULD BRING ME TO A PLACE LIKE SOUTH KOREA. AND NOW, AS I FELL IN LOVE WITH SEO JUN, I KNEW THAT I HAD TO CHOOSE BETWEEN MY CAREER AND MY HEART.

TO BE CONTINUED...

ABOUT AUTHOR

MEET THE *CREATOR* BEHIND THE STORY

WWW.LIFEACCORDINGTOLASHAI.COM

Shai (aka Lashai Ben Salmi) is a Multi Award-Winning Author, TEDx Speaker, Founder (of Hallyu Con), Publisher, Creator, International Relations & Cultural Connectivity Advocate and Youth Advocate, UN Women UK Delegate & Distinguished Korean Wave Representative (a title and award presented to her by the Director of the Korean Cultural Centre UK due to her extensive work and contributions to the promotion of the Korean Wave). Shai is one of the most prominent and influential names in the Hallyu sector, strengthening relations between the UK and South Korea.

She can be seen featured on/in The Korea Times, Korea.Net (where she was given an award - presented by the First Lady Of South Korea), BBC Korea, MBC, KTO, Virgin Money, Yonhap News and on BBC Sounds, starring in their BBC Radio 1 series "K-Pop: A Stan Story", where she was featured (as a Hallyu expert due to being a cultural connectivity advocate) alongside the likes of Johnny Suh from NCT and KANGTA.

Follow The Story @AFamiliarAura

BOOK 2
Sneak PEEK

LOOK AT THE TV
AALIYAH, THAT'S HIM!
POINTS AT THE TV*
YOU ARE MY DESTINY
TVM
YOU ARE MY DESTINY

I FROZE, SHOCKED TO REALIZE THAT THE BOY WHO WAS SO KIND TO ME DURING MY TIME AT THE KIDS CLUB WAS THE SAME PERSON THAT WAS NOW CAUSING MY HEART TO WONDER.
XXXX AGED 14*

„ THE HEART
NEVER FORGETS

SCAN THIS QR
CODE TO UNLOCK
THE AURA PLAYLIST

WRITTEN BY **SHAI**

a familiar

AURA

THE HEART NEVER FORGETS

A **DREAM** THAT BROUGHT HER TO **SEOUL. A CONNECTION** SHE **NEVER EXPECTED.** A **CHOICE** THAT COULD **CHANGE EVERYTHING.**

IN **'A FAMILIAR AURA: THE HEART NEVER FORGETS'** (VOLUME 1), WE FOLLOW THE JOURNEY OF AALIYAH, A HALF-KOREAN ACTRESS FROM LONDON, AS SHE PURSUES HER DREAMS OF ACTING INTERNATIONALLY. THIS DREAM UNEXPECTEDLY LEADS HER TO SEOUL, SOUTH KOREA. AS SHE IMMERSES HERSELF IN THE CULTURE AND TRADITIONS OF HER MOTHER'S HOMELAND, SHE FINDS HERSELF DRAWN TO HER CHARISMATIC AND POPULAR CO-STAR, **SEO JUN.** BUT AS THESE FEELINGS DEEPEN, **AALIYAH MUST CHOOSE BETWEEN** HER CAREER AND HER HEART. WILL AALIYAH FOLLOW **HER DREAMS,** HER HEART OR PERHAPS SOMETHING NEW?..

FIND OUT IN **'A FAMILIAR AURA:** THE HEART NEVER FORGETS' (VOLUME 1), A HEARTWARMING TALE OF LOVE, CAREER, AND FINDING ONESELF IN A NEW PLACE.